Joan G. Robinson was born in Buckinghamshire in 1910. She studied at the Chelsea Illustrators' Studio and then went on to write and illustrate many books, of which the *Teddy Robinson* and *Mary-Mary* books are amongst the most well known. Joan Robinson was married with two daughters. She died in 1988.

Joan G. Robinson

ABOUT TEDDY ROBINSON

PUFFIN BOOKS

PUFFIN BOOKS

Published by the Penguin Group
Penguin Books Ltd, 27 Wrights Lane, London W8 5TZ, England
Penguin Putnam Inc., 375 Hudson Street, New York,
New York 10014, USA
Penguin Books Australia Ltd, Ringwood, Victoria, Australia
Penguin Books Canada Ltd, 10 Alcorn Avenue, Toronto,
Ontario, Canada M4V 3B2
Penguin Books (NZ) Ltd, Cnr Rosedale and Airborne Roads, Albany,
Auckland, New Zealand

Penguin Books Ltd, Registered Offices: Harmondsworth,
Middlesex, England

First published by George G. Harrap & Co. Ltd, in *Teddy Robinson's
Omnibus* 1959
Published in Puffin Books as *More About Teddy Robinson* 1970
Reprinted as *About Teddy Robinson* 1974
15 17 19 20 18 16

Set in Monotype Imprint

Made and printed in England by Clays Ltd, St Ives plc

British Library Cataloguing in Publication Data
A CIP catalogue record for this book is available from
the British Library

ISBN 0–140–30752–4

Contents

1 Teddy Robinson's Night Out   7
2 Teddy Robinson goes to Hospital   17
3 Teddy Robinson is a Red Indian   29
4 Teddy Robinson goes to the Fair   41
5 Teddy Robinson gets Lost   55
6 Teddy Robinson meets Father Christmas   64
7 Teddy Robinson has a Birthday Party   77
8 Teddy Robinson and Toby   92
9 Teddy Robinson is put in a Book   105

For
Gregory
Barnaby
Mungo
Jessamy

and everyone who
has a Teddy Bear

I

Teddy Robinson's Night Out

TEDDY ROBINSON was a nice, big, comfortable, friendly teddy bear. He had light brown fur and kind brown eyes, and he belonged to a little girl called Deborah. He was Deborah's favourite teddy bear, and Deborah was Teddy Robinson's favourite little girl, so they got on very well together, and wherever one of them went the other one usually went too.

One Saturday afternoon Teddy Robinson and Deborah looked out of the window and saw that the sun was shining and the almond-tree in the garden was covered with pink blossom.

'That's nice,' said Deborah. 'We can play out there. We will make our house under the little pink tree, and you can get brown in the sun, Teddy Robinson.'

So she took out a little tray with the dolls' tea-set on it, and a blanket to sit on, and the toy telephone in case anyone rang them up, and she laid all the things out on the grass under the tree. Then she fetched a colouring book and some chalks for herself, and a book of nursery rhymes for Teddy Robinson.

Deborah lay on her tummy and coloured the whole of an elephant and half a Noah's ark, and Teddy Robinson

*He stared hard
at a picture of Humpty-Dumpty*

stared hard at a picture of Humpty-Dumpty and tried
to remember the words. He couldn't really read, but he
loved pretending to.

'Hump, hump, humpety-hump,' he said to himself
over and over again; and then, 'Hump, hump, humpety-
hump, Deborah's drawing an elephump.'

'Oh, Teddy Robinson,' said Deborah, 'don't think so
loud – I can't hear myself chalking.' Then, seeing him
still bending over his book, she said, 'Poor boy, I expect
you're tired. It's time for your rest now.' And she laid
him down flat on his back so that he could look up into
the sky.

At that moment there was a loud *rat-tat* on the front
door and a long ring on the door-bell. Deborah jumped
up and ran indoors to see who it could be, and Teddy
Robinson lay back and began to count the number of

blossoms he could see in the almond-tree. He couldn't count more than four because he only had two arms and two legs to count on, so he counted up to four a great many times over, and then he began counting backward, and the wrong way round, and any way round that he could think of, and sometimes he put words in between his counting, so that in the end it went something like this:

'One, two, three, four,
some one knocking at the door.
One, four three, two,
open the door and how d'you do?
Four, two, three, one,
isn't it nice to lie in the sun?
One, two, four, three,
underneath the almond-tree.'

And he was very happy counting and singing to himself for quite a long time.

Then Teddy Robinson noticed that the sun was going down and there were long shadows in the garden. It looked as if it must be getting near bedtime.

Deborah will come and fetch me soon, he thought; and he watched the birds flying home to their nests in the trees above him.

A blackbird flew quite close to him and whistled and chirped, 'Good night, teddy bear.'

'Good night, bird,' said Teddy Robinson and waved an arm at him.

Then a snail came crawling past.

'Are you sleeping out tonight? That will be nice for you,' he said. 'Good night, teddy bear.'

'Good night, snail,' said Teddy Robinson, and he watched it crawl slowly away into the long grass.

She will come and fetch me soon, he thought. It must be getting quite late.

But Deborah didn't come and fetch him. Do you know why? She was fast asleep in bed!

This is what had happened. When she had run to see who was knocking at the front door, Deborah had found Uncle Michael standing on the doorstep. He had come in his new car, and he said there was just time to take her out for a ride if she came quickly, but she must hurry because he had to get into the town before tea-time. There was only just time for Mummy to get Deborah's coat on and wave good-bye before they were off. They had come home ever so much later than they meant to because they had tea out in a shop, and then on the way home the new car had suddenly stopped and it took Uncle Michael a long time to find out what was wrong with it.

By the time they reached home Deborah was half asleep, and Mummy had bundled her into bed before she had time to really wake up again and remember about Teddy Robinson still being in the garden.

He didn't know all this, of course, but he guessed

The garden tortoise came tramping slowly past

something unusual must have happened to make Deborah forget about him.

Soon a little wind blew across the garden, and down fluttered some blossom from the almond-tree. It fell right in the middle of Teddy Robinson's tummy.

'Thank you,' he said, 'I like pink flowers for a blanket.'

So the almond-tree shook its branches again, and more and more blossoms came tumbling down.

The garden tortoise came tramping slowly past.

'Hallo, teddy bear,' he said. 'Are you sleeping out? I hope you won't be cold. I felt a little breeze blowing up just now. I'm glad I've got my house with me.'

'But I have a fur coat,' said Teddy Robinson, 'and pink blossom for a blanket.'

'So you have,' said the tortoise. 'That's lucky. Well,

good night,' and he drew his head into his shell and went to sleep close by.

The next-door kitten came padding softly through the grass and rubbed against him gently.

'You *are* out late,' she said.

'Yes, I think I'm sleeping out tonight,' said Teddy Robinson.

'Are you?' said the kitten. 'You'll love that. I did it once, I'm going to do it a lot oftener when I'm older. Perhaps I'll stay out tonight.'

But just then a window opened in the house next door and a voice called, 'Puss! Puss! Puss! Come and have your fish! fish! fish!' and the kitten scampered off as fast as she could go.

Teddy Robinson heard the window shut down and then everything was quiet again.

The sky grew darker and darker blue, and soon the stars came out. Teddy Robinson lay and stared at them without blinking, and they twinkled and shone and winked at him as if they were surprised to see a teddy bear lying in the garden.

And after a while they began to sing to him, a very soft and sweet and far-away little song, to the tune of *Rock-a-Bye Baby*, and it went something like this:

'Rock-a-bye Teddy, go to sleep soon.
We will be watching, so will the moon.
When you awake with dew on your paws
Down will come Debbie and take you indoors.'

'Would you like a worm for your breakfast?'

Teddy Robinson thought that was a lovely song, so when it was finished he sang one back to them. He sang it in a grunty voice because he was rather shy, and it went something like this:

> "This is me
> under the tree,
> the bravest bear you ever did see.
> All alone
> so brave I've grown,
> I'm camping out on my very own.'

The stars nodded and winked and twinkled to show that they liked Teddy Robinson's song, and then they sang *Rock-a-bye Teddy* all over again, and he stared and stared at them until he fell asleep.

She picked him up and hugged him.

Very early in the morning a blackbird whistled, then another blackbird answered, and then all the birds in the garden opened their beaks and twittered and cheeped and sang. And Teddy Robinson woke up.

One of the blackbirds hopped up with a worm in his beak.

'Good morning, teddy bear,' he said. 'Would you like a worm for your breakfast?'

'Oh, no, thank you,' said Teddy Robinson. 'I don't usually bother about breakfast. Do eat it yourself.'

'Thank you, I will,' said the blackbird, and he gobbled it up and hopped off to find some more.

Then the snail came slipping past.

'Good morning, teddy bear,' he said. 'Did you sleep well?'

'Oh, yes, thank you,' said Teddy Robinson.

The next-door kitten came scampering up, purring.

'You lucky pur-r-son,' she said as she rubbed against Teddy Robinson. 'Your fur-r is damp but it was a pur-r-fect night for staying out. I didn't want to miss my fish supper last night, otherwise I'd have stayed with you. Pur-r-haps I will another night. Did you enjoy it?'

'Oh, yes,' said Teddy Robinson. 'You were quite right about sleeping out. It was lovely.'

The tortoise poked his head out and blinked.

'Hallo,' he said. 'There's a lot of talking going on for so early in the morning. What is it all about? Oh, good morning, bear. I'd forgotten you were here. I hope you had a comfortable night.' And before Teddy Robinson could answer he had popped back inside his shell.

Then a moment later Teddy Robinson heard a little shuffling noise in the grass behind him, and there was Deborah out in the garden with bare feet, and in her pyjamas!

She picked him up and hugged him and kissed him and whispered to him very quietly, and then she ran through the wet grass and in at the kitchen door and up the stairs into her own room. A minute later she and

Teddy Robinson were snuggled down in her warm little bed.

'You poor, poor boy,' she whispered as she stroked his damp fur. 'I never meant to leave you out all night. Oh, you poor, poor boy.'

But Teddy Robinson whispered back, 'I aren't a poor boy at all. I was camping out, and it was lovely.' And then he tried to tell her all about the blackbird, and the snail, and the tortoise, and the kitten, and the stars. But because it was really so very early in the morning, and Deborah's bed was really so very warm and cosy, they both got drowsy; and before he had even got to the part about the stars singing their song to him both Teddy Robinson and Deborah were fast asleep.

And that is the end of the story about how Teddy Robinson stayed out all night.

2

Teddy Robinson goes to Hospital

ONCE upon a time Teddy Robinson and Deborah went to hospital. They didn't know a bit what it was going to be like because neither of them had ever been before, so they were glad to have each other for company.

A kind nurse in a white cap and apron tucked them up in a little white bed in a big room called the ward, and while Mummy was in another room talking to the doctor they lay side by side and whispered to each other, and looked around to see what hospital was like.

There were a lot of other children in the ward as well. Some of them were in little white beds like Deborah and Teddy Robinson, and some of them were dressed and running around in soft bedroom slippers.

There were coloured pictures of nursery rhyme people all round the walls, and quite close to Deborah's bed there was a big glass tank full of water with a lot of tiny fish swimming around inside. It was called an aquarium.

Teddy Robinson liked this, and so did Deborah. After a while they sat up so that they could see better, and they watched the fish swimming round and round until Mummy came in to say good-bye.

They were rather sad to say good-bye, but Mummy

'Been here long?'

promised she would come and see them again next day, and when she had gone Deborah comforted Teddy Robinson, and Teddy Robinson comforted Deborah, and a nice kind nurse came and comforted them both, so they didn't need to be sad after all.

A little boy in the next bed said, 'What's your name? I'm called Tommy. Would your bear like to talk to my horse?' And he pulled out a little brown felt horse from under the blanket and threw it over to Deborah's bed.

'His name's Cloppety,' he said.

'Thank you,' said Deborah. 'My name is Deborah, and this is Teddy Robinson,' and she sat them side by side with their noses close together so they they could make friends with each other.

Teddy Robinson and Cloppety stared hard at each other for quite a long while, then they began to talk quietly.

'Been here long?' asked Teddy Robinson.

'About a week,' said Cloppety. 'We're going home soon because Tommy's nearly better; he's getting up tomorrow. Why are you only wearing a vest?'

'I don't know,' said Teddy Robinson. 'Deborah forgot my trousers.'

'What a pity,' said Cloppety. 'I had to leave my cart at home, so I know what it feels like. Are you happy here?'

'Yes,' said Teddy Robinson, 'I like watching the fish.'

'So do I,' said Cloppety.

When evening came and all the children were tucked up for the night it was very cosy in the ward. Little lights were left burning so that it was never quite dark, and Teddy Robinson and Deborah lay and watched the nurses going round to all the beds and cots and tucking up each of the children in turn. Cloppety had gone back to Tommy's bed, so they snuggled down together just as they did at home.

'Dear old boy,' said Deborah. 'I'm glad you're with me. Isn't Tommy a nice boy?'

'Yes,' said Teddy Robinson, 'and Cloppety's a nice horse.'

And quite soon they were both fast asleep.

The next day Tommy was up, and running around in bedroom slippers like the other children who were nearly better, so for quite a lot of the day Cloppety stayed with Teddy Robinson, and Tommy came to see

Deborah every now and then, and brought her toys and books from the hospital toy cupboard.

Mummy came to see them, and she brought a red shoulder-bag with a zip-fastener for Deborah, and a real little nightshirt (made out of Deborah's old pyjamas) for Teddy Robinson. She also brought his old trousers that had got left behind by mistake.

They were very pleased. Deborah wore the shoulder-bag sitting up in bed, and Teddy Robinson put on his new nightie straight away.

'That's nice,' said Cloppety, peeping over the bed-clothes when Mummy had gone.

'Yes,' said Teddy Robinson. 'It's just what I was needing. Do you wish you had one?'

'Horses don't bother with nighties,' said Cloppety. 'I wish you could have seen my cart, though. It's green with yellow wheels, and the wheels really go round.'

But Teddy Robinson wasn't listening. He was beginning to make up a little song in his head, all about his new nightie. And this is how it went:

> 'Highty tiddly ighty,
> a teddy bear wearing a nightie
> can feel he's dressed
> and looking his best
> (he couldn't do that in only a vest),
> highty tiddly ighty.'

In a few days the doctor said Deborah was better, and she was allowed to get up and run about the ward with the other children who were dressed; but Teddy Robinson still liked his nightie so much better than his vest and trousers that he decided he wasn't well enough to get up yet.

'Shall I dress you, too, Teddy Robinson?' asked Deborah.

'No, thank you,' he said. 'I think I'll stay in my nightie and sit on the pillow. I can watch you from there, and it will rest my legs.'

The next day Tommy went home because he was quite well again, and Teddy Robinson and Deborah were quite sorry when he and Cloppety came to say good-bye. All the rest of that day his bed looked so empty that they didn't like looking at it.

'Never mind, Teddy Robinson,' said Deborah. 'We'll be going home ourselves soon.' And they went off together to play with the other children.

Those who were up and nearly better had their meals at a little table at the other end of the ward, so it wasn't until after tea that Teddy Robinson and Deborah came back to their own bed. When they did they were surprised to see a new little girl lying in Tommy's bed.

'Hallo,' said Deborah. 'You weren't here before tea.'

'No,' said the little girl. 'I've only just come, and I want to go home,' and she looked as if she might be going to cry.

So Deborah said, 'I expect you *will* go home soon.

But it's nice here.' And then she told her all about the hospital, and showed her the aquarium, and the little girl told her that her name was Betty, and soon they were quite like best friends.

'I wish I'd brought my doll,' said Betty, looking at Teddy Robinson. 'I came in a hurry and forgot her. Mummy's going to bring her tomorrow, but I want her now,' and she looked as if she might cry again.

'You'd better have my teddy for a little while,' said Deborah. 'He's nice to cuddle if you're feeling sad. But don't cry all over his fur. He doesn't like it.'

So Teddy Robinson got into bed beside Betty. He didn't talk to her because he was shy and didn't know her, but Betty seemed to like him and soon her eyes closed and she fell asleep hugging him.

When it was Deborah's bed-time she didn't like to take Teddy Robinson back in case she woke Betty, so she asked the nurse who came to tuck her up. The nurse went over to Betty's bed and looked at her and then she came back to Deborah.

'Would you mind very much if she kept him just for tonight?' she said. 'She is fast asleep, and it seems such a pity to wake her. It would be awfully kind if you could lend him.'

So Deborah said she would, and Teddy Robinson stayed where he was.

Deborah soon dropped off to sleep, but Teddy Robinson didn't. He lay in Betty's bed and watched the night-

nurse who was writing at a little table, and looked at the
fish swimming round and round in the aquarium, and
then he began to sing to himself very softly, and after a
while when he was sure that all the children were asleep
he rolled over, tumbled gently out of bed, and rolled
a little way across the floor.

At that moment a baby in a cot woke up and began
to cry. The night-nurse stopped writing and came
quickly down the ward to see who it was. As she passed
Teddy Robinson her foot bumped against him and she
nearly fell over him. She bent down and picked him up
and then hurried on to comfort the crying baby.

As soon as the baby saw Teddy Robinson he stopped
crying and said, 'Teddy, teddy,' so the nurse put Teddy
Robinson inside the cot and let the baby hold him. But
when she tried to take him back the baby started crying
again, so after a while the nurse left him there, hoping
he would help the baby go to sleep, and she went back
to her writing.

But the baby didn't go to sleep. Instead he began
pulling Teddy Robinson's arms and legs and ears, and
poking his fingers in his eyes. Teddy Robinson didn't
mind much because it didn't hurt him, but after a while
the baby pulled his right ear so that it nearly came off,
and instead of sticking up on top of his head like the
other ear it hung down with only a thread of cotton
holding it on.

'I bet I look silly,' he said to himself. 'I wonder

—peeping through the bars with one ear
hanging right down—

what Deborah will say.' And he felt rather sorry about it.

In the morning when the children all woke up Deborah and Betty didn't know wherever Teddy Robinson could be. They looked everywhere in both their beds, but of course they couldn't find him. So as soon as she was dressed Deborah began going round the ward looking at all the children's beds and peeping into all the babies' cots. And when she came to the cot where he was she could hardly believe it!

The baby was fast asleep at last, but there was poor Teddy Robinson peeping through the bars with one ear hanging right down over his eye.

'You poor old boy,' she said. 'What *are* you doing in there? You look as if you're in a cage. Wait a minute and I'll get you out.'

She had to ask a nurse to lift him out of the cot, and then she hugged him and kissed him and carried him back to her own bed.

'Oh, Teddy Robinson,' she said, 'how did you get there? And what *has* happened to your poor ear? It's only hanging on by one little piece of cotton.'

'I think you'd better pull it off,' said Teddy Robinson bravely, 'otherwise I might lose it.'

'All right,' said Deborah, 'and I'll keep it for you till we get home; then we'll ask Mummy to mend it.'

Then she gave the ear a sharp little tug and off it came.

'You're a dear brave boy,' said Deborah, and she

kissed the place where it had been, and put the ear carefully away in her shoulder-bag.

When the night-nurse came round that evening and saw Teddy Robinson sitting on the pillow with only one ear she remembered what had happened the night before, and she told Deborah all about it; how she had nearly fallen over him and had given him to the baby to stop him crying.

'But I *am* sorry about his ear,' she said.

'It's all right,' said Deborah. 'I've got it safely in my shoulder-bag, and we're going home tomorrow, so Mummy will mend it.'

'I'm so glad,' said the nurse. 'I was wondering if he would like it bandaged.'

Deborah knew that Teddy Robinson would simply love that, so she said, 'Oh, yes, please!' And the nurse bandaged Teddy Robinson's head round and round with a piece of real hospital bandage. He didn't mind a bit that one eye got covered up at the same time, and when it was finished both Deborah and the nurse said he looked lovely.

Early next morning Teddy Robinson was dressed in his vest and trousers again, and his nightie was packed away with his ear in Deborah's shoulder-bag. Mummy came to fetch them, and they said good-bye to everybody, even the fish in the aquarium.

They were both very pleased to be going home again, and Teddy Robinson was specially pleased because he

She bandaged his head

was going out with a real bandage on. He couldn't help hoping that everyone would notice it, because then they would all know that he had been in a real hospital!

And that is the end of the story about how Teddy Robinson went to hospital.

Teddy Robinson is a Red Indian.

3

Teddy Robinson is a Red Indian

ONE day a boy came to stay with Deborah and Teddy
Robinson. His name was Philip, and he was Deborah's
cousin. He brought a big suitcase with him because he
had come to stay for a whole week. Deborah and Teddy
Robinson watched while Mummy helped him to un-
pack.

When they had taken out all the socks and pullovers
and pyjamas and were getting near the bottom of the
suitcase, they began to find some really interesting
things.

First there was a Red Indian suit.

'I had it for my birthday,' said Philip.

Then two feather headdresses.

'I brought them both, in case you hadn't got one,'
said Philip. 'We might want to play Red Indians.' Then
there were a bow and arrow, and a little bundle of
pigeon's feathers, and right at the bottom of the case,
rolled up in a bundle, was a real Red Indian tent.

'That is my wigwam,' said Philip. 'It's quite big
enough for both of us to get inside.'

'Oh, it's lovely!' said Deborah. 'Can we put it up in
the garden?'

'Yes, of course,' said Philip. 'That's what I brought it for.'

'But not tonight,' said Mummy. 'It's nearly bedtime already, and we haven't had tea yet. You must wait until tomorrow.'

Teddy Robinson was very interested in all this. He thought there was nothing he would like better than to be a Red Indian and sit inside a wigwam, and he hoped Deborah would remind Philip about him.

But Philip was a nice boy and didn't need reminding. As soon as he saw Teddy Robinson he said, 'Hallo, you're just the kind of bear I like.' And Teddy Robinson was very pleased because Philip was just the kind of boy *he* liked. He could whistle, he could make a noise like an aeroplane with his mouth, he walked about with his hands in his pockets, and he seemed to Teddy Robinson quite the biggest and bravest boy he had ever seen.

He began to practice making aeroplane noises himself, and wished Mummy had thought of putting pockets in his trousers. 'I should like to be as big and as brave as Philip,' he said to himself.

As soon as breakfast was finished the next day, Deborah said, 'Can we put up the tent now?'

And Philip said, 'Yes. We'll be Red Indians. Let's go down into the forest and hunt wild animals.'

'Oh, yes, let's!' said Deborah. 'Where is the forest?'

He had a doll's blanket wrapped round him

'Down at the bottom of your garden,' said Philip, 'where those bushes are. We can make our camp there.'

'Oh, yes!' said Deborah. 'What fun!'

'Teddy Robinson can come too if he wants,' said Philip. 'He can guard the wigwam.'

'Hooray,' said Teddy Robinson to himself. 'That's just what I was hoping would happen.'

So Philip put on his Red Indian suit and one feather headdress, and Deborah put on a pair of pyjama trousers and the other feather headdress, and Teddy Robinson had a red doll's blanket wrapped round him and fastened with a safety-pin. Then they all went off to the forest at the bottom of the garden.

'This is a good place for the wigwam,' said Philip. 'We'll put it here. Hurry and help me get it up, Debbie.'

I can hear some lions and tigers prowling about already.'

Teddy Robinson's fur began to feel as if it was standing up on end, but Deborah whispered to him, 'It's all right, we're only pretending,' and then his fur felt smooth again.

'Now,' said Philip, 'I'm a Red Indian brave and I've got to go and hunt those wild animals. You can be a squaw, Debbie.'

'I don't know what that is,' said Deborah, 'but I'd rather be a Red Indian too.'

'All right,' said Philip. 'We'll be two Red Indians and Teddy Robinson can be the squaw.'

'I don't think he wants to be the squaw either. Do you, Teddy Robinson?' said Deborah.

'No,' said Teddy Robinson. 'If I'm going to guard the wam-wig I'd better be a Red Indian too.'

'That's what I think,' said Deborah. 'But it's not a wam-wig, it's a wig-wam.'

'All right,' said Teddy Robinson. 'I'll call it a tent It's easier.'

'Now, how can we make you look like a Red Indian?' said Deborah. 'The blanket's all right, but you need something on your head.'

'I know!' said Philip. 'I've got three pigeons' feathers he can have. Lend me your hair ribbon, Debbie.'

So Debbie took off her hair ribbon, and Philip tied it

He sat up very straight and practised growling

round Teddy Robinson's head; then he stuck the three
feathers inside at the front.

'That looks fine,' said Deborah. 'You look like a real
Red Indian now.'

'Good,' said Teddy Robinson. 'That's just what I
feel like.'

'Now,' said Philip, 'we're going off to hunt. You sit
here in the doorway, and remember that if any lions or
tigers or grizzly bears come by you're to drive them
away.'

'All right,' said Teddy Robinson. 'Good-bye.'

When Philip and Deborah had gone Teddy Robinson

settled down to really enjoy being a Red Indian. He sat up very straight with his tummy sticking out and practised growling and making fierce noises.

Then he began to look around to see if there were any wild animals creeping about. As he looked he saw the top leaves of the hedge moving about in the wind.

Now, that's just how a hedge would move, he thought, if a lion were walking quietly by on the other side. So he growled fiercely to frighten it away; and a moment later, when the wind stopped blowing, the top leaves of the hedge stopped moving.

'That's *one* wild animal gone.' said Teddy Robinson, and felt very brave.

Then he looked at the tool-shed which stood in a corner of the garden.

That's the place a grizzly bear would choose to hide behind, he thought, if he happened to be in the garden and didn't want me to see him.

So he growled again and said, 'Boo-yah-boo!' as loudly as he could.

Nothing came out from behind the tool-shed.

'Good,' said Teddy Robinson. 'That's frightened *him* away.' He was glad to think there were two wild animals less in the garden.

He began to feel rather proud of himself, and sat in the doorway of the tent waving his arms and making up a song about how brave he was.

'you _are_ brave!'

'I'm a brave,
I'm a brave,
see how fiercely I behave!
Hear me growl
and hear me shout!
Watch me wave my arms about!
Did *anybody* *ever* see
a Fiercer, Braver Bear than Me?'

Just then he heard a creeping, rustling noise in the grass behind the tent, and then the pad-pad of feet coming nearer and nearer.

Teddy Robinson knew he ought to growl and be fierce again, but he was rather out of breath with singing his brave song, and anyway he wanted to know who was coming before he drove them away. So he held his breath and decided to look tame until he knew who it was.

A moment later the next-door kitten came round the corner of the tent.

'Hallo,' said the kitten in a gentle, purring voice. 'I haven't seen *you* for a long, long while.'

'Oh, it's you,' said Teddy Robinson. 'I thought you were a wild animal.'

'Did you *really*?' said the next-door kitten, rather pleased.

'Well, only for a minute,' said Teddy Robinson, 'otherwise I'd have driven you away. I'm a Red Indian, and I'm guarding the tent. I wonder, would you mind going back where you came from, and coming round the corner of the tent again? You see, I wasn't quite expecting you before, so I wasn't as fierce as I should have been.'

'Oh, yes, cer-r-r-tainly,' purred the kitten. 'I'll be a tiger,' and she scampered off very pleased.

Next time she came round the corner of the tent Teddy Robinson was ready for her, and as soon as he saw her he began to growl and shout and make very fierce noises indeed.

The next-door kitten was quite surprised. She looked at him with big round eyes and said, 'You *are* brave!'

'Yes, aren't I?' said Teddy Robinson. 'I've tamed you now, so you can come into the tent and lie down.'

'Thank you,' said the kitten, and she stepped into the tent and began to wash her paws.

Teddy Robinson looked out to see what else there was that might need taming or driving away; but there were only a few pigeons walking about on the lawn. They were pecking at the grass, and after a while they came strutting down towards the tent and began to look at Teddy Robinson, and to whisper about him.

He took no notice.

'After all, they're only pigeons,' he said to himself, 'not wild animals.'

So the pigeons came nearer and began to whisper louder.

'Coo! Look at *him*!' they said. 'He's wearing pigeons' feathers and trying to make himself look like one of us. Coo! Coo! That will never do!'

Teddy Robinson began to get cross.

'I'm *not* trying to look like a pigeon!' he shouted. 'Go away!'

'Coo! Coo!' said the pigeons. 'It's only a teddy bear dressed up.'

Teddy Robinson turned round and called softly to the next-door kitten. She had finished washing her paws, and was curled up in the tent asleep.

'Tiger!' he said. 'Do you mind waking up and coming over here?'

The kitten trotted up to him.

'Would you like to forget you are tame for a minute,' said Teddy Robinson, 'and chase those pigeons away?'

'Here we sit on guard together—'

'Oh, *yes*!' said the kitten, and pounced out of the tent.
And as soon as they saw her every one of the pigeons
flapped his wings and flew away.

'Well done!' said Teddy Robinson. 'You're jolly
good at frightening pigeons away. I'm rather better at
wild animals myself.'

'Yes,' said the kitten, 'we're both rather fierce really,
aren't we? It's a good job we're here to guard the tent.
Shall we purr a song about it?'

'Oh, yes!' said Teddy Robinson. 'But I'll growl if
you don't mind. I'm not very good at purring. Shall we
each make up a line in turn?'

'Yes, but I'll have the first line,' said the kitten,
'because I thought of it first.'

'All right,' said Teddy Robinson, 'and we'll both sing the last line together.'

And this is the song they sang:

> 'I'm a tiger in his lair.'
> 'I'm a brave Red Indian bear.'
> 'One in fur —'
> 'And one in feather —'
> 'Here we sit on guard together.'

'I think that's rather good, don't you?' they said, nodding their heads at each other. 'Let's sing it again.'

After they had sung the song four times the kitten curled up and went to sleep, and Teddy Robinson leaned against the tent thinking how nice it was to be a fierce Red Indian having a quiet little rest.

He was nearly dropping off to sleep himself when back came Philip and Deborah.

'Hallo,' they said. 'Did you guard the tent well?'

'Yes,' said Teddy Robinson. 'I drove away a lion and a grizzly bear that were too frightened even to let me see them; and this is a tiger that I've tamed.'

'Well, you *are* a brave chap!' said Philip.

'I know I are,' said Teddy Robinson.

But much later on, when they had finished being Red Indians and he and Deborah were sitting alone together for a minute, Teddy Robinson said, 'Perhaps I ought to tell you that the lion and the grizzly bear that I drove away *might* not have been there.'

'No,' said Deborah. 'I don't suppose they were.'

'But I did like Philip calling me brave,' said Teddy Robinson.

'Of course you did,' said Deborah. 'And I think you *were* brave, even if they weren't there. You're the Best and Biggest, most Beautiful Brave Brown Bear that ever I saw,' she said, and hugged him.

And that is the end of the story about how Teddy Robinson was a Red Indian.

4

Teddy Robinson goes to the Fair

ONE day Teddy Robinson sat on the window-sill of Deborah's room and thought about all the things he most specially wanted. Deborah was helping Mummy to bake a gingerbread man that morning, so he had a nice long time to think.

First he thought how jolly it would be if a fairy came by and asked him to go to tea with the Man in the Moon. But that was only pretend thinking, and he knew it couldn't really happen so he decided to think about real things instead. He found there were quite a lot of real things he wanted.

I would like to be able to play the piano, he thought, then I could make the music for the songs I think of; and he had a picture in his mind of how nice he would look sitting up at the piano on a high stool, while everybody sat round listening to him playing.

Then I want a satchel, he thought, and a pair of Wellington boots, and I would like to ride on a horse; but, more than all the other things, what I *most* specially want is to drive a motor-car.

He had often been for rides on buses with Deborah, and when they had been lucky enough to have the front

He had a picture in his mind of how nice he would look sitting up at the piano

seat on top he had done quite a lot of things to help the driver make the bus start and stop. He had found that when the traffic lights were changing from red to yellow he had only to push forward once or twice and the bus would start. And when the traffic lights were changing from green back to yellow and red all he had to do was to sit back sharply and the bus would stop.

But, of course, that was not the same as really driving. It was only helping.

'I must practise driving a motor-car all by myself,' he said, 'just in case I ever have the chance.'

So he sat on the window-sill and rocked gently from side to side, growling to make a motor-car noise. Then he held the middle button of his jacket between his paws and turned it round, first this way and then that, to practise going round corners. He had just decided that he was now good enough at driving to take himself for a long pretend ride before dinner, when Deborah came running into the room.

'Guess what, Teddy Robinson!' she said. 'The fair has come, and we're going this afternoon!'

To practise going round corners

'Good,' said Teddy Robinson. 'In that case I won't go for a pretend ride after all. What is a fair?'

'Oh, it's lovely,' said Deborah. 'There are swings and roundabouts and all sorts of things. You shall come for a ride with me.'

'What on?' asked Teddy Robinson.

'On a horse on the roundabout,' said Deborah.

'Oh, *very* nice,' said Teddy Robinson. 'That's one of the things I was specially wanting.'

While Deborah brushed his fur with the doll's brush, and put on his best purple dress that he always wore for parties, Teddy Robinson began to sing to himself because he was so happy:

> "The fair, the fair,
> we're off to the fair.
> What shall we do when we get there?
> Ride, of course,
> on a galloping horse;
> a nice little girl and a Big Brown Bear.'

'Don't be silly,' said Deborah. 'It ought to be a big girl and a middling-sized bear.'

'It sounded better the other way,' said Teddy Robinson, 'and anyway I always feel big when I'm happy.'

After dinner they all set off.

Mummy had given Deborah two shillings to spend at the fair, and she and Teddy Robinson were busy all the way there thinking how they were going to spend it.

The music began and off they went

'It will make four rides if they are sixpence each.' said Mummy.

'Or three rides and one candy floss,' said Deborah.

'Or four candy flosses?' said Teddy Robinson.

'Yes, but they're so big we shan't want four,' said Deborah.

'Shan't we?' said Teddy Robinson. 'What are they?'

'They're great big fluffy things on sticks,' said Deborah. 'They look like pink cotton-wool, but you can eat them.'

Soon they heard the noise of the fair music, and a

moment later they turned the corner and were in the fairground.

Teddy Robinson thought he had never seen anything so exciting. There were so many things to look at that he didn't know which to look at first. But Deborah decided for him.

'Look, Teddy Robinson,' she said. 'There's the roundabout with the horses. Shall we go on that first?'

'Oh, yes,' he said.

So they waited for the roundabout to stop and then ran to choose their horse. It was a beautiful roundabout, all painted in red and gold, and each of the horses had its own name painted on its side.

'Can I have a horse to myself?' asked Teddy Robinson.

'No, you might fall off,' said Deborah, 'and anyway we'd have to pay extra.'

So they chose a grey and white spotted horse called Nellie, and climbed up on to her back together. Teddy Robinson sat in front with his paws round Nellie's neck. 'Don't hold me, then,' he said.

'All right,' said Deborah. Then the music began and off they went. Mummy stood and watched them as they went by. Teddy Robinson didn't dare wave back in case he fell off, and as they went faster and faster he was glad to feel that Deborah was holding him after all. It was most exciting. He began to sing his little fair song again, but this time he changed it to

"Shall we be able to eat it all today?"

'Gee up, Nellie, to the fair,
round and round till we get there;
gallop along as fast as you dare
with the nice little girl and the Big Brown Bear.'

When the music stopped and the horses stood still
again they felt they couldn't bear to get down just yet,
so they stayed on Nellie for another ride. Deborah gave
the man another sixpence and off they went again.

It was just as lovely as the first ride, but it seemed
even shorter. Next time the horses stopped they said
good-bye to Nellie and climbed down.

'Thank you,' said Teddy Robinson. 'That was very
nice.'

After that they went to the candy-floss stall. They
gave the lady sixpence, and she made them a candy floss
that was nearly as big as Teddy Robinson.

'Good gracious!' he said. 'Shall we be able to eat it
all today?'

But though it looked so big it was very fluffy, and it
didn't take them long to eat their way right through it.

'We've only got sixpence left already,' said Deborah
when they had finished. 'We'd better go and look at
some other things before we decide what to spend it on.'

They stopped at a stall where some people were
throwing darts at a board.

'What are they doing that for?' asked Deborah.

'If they get a big enough number they win a prize,'
said Mummy.

Deborah and Teddy Robinson decided they would save their last sixpence for something else, but they stayed for a while to watch.

At the back of the stall were the prizes. There were a lot of tea-sets and glass dishes and some baskets of fruit, and standing up in the middle were five very large pale blue teddy bears. They were wrapped in cellophane and looked beautifully new and shiny, but they had rather silly faces.

Teddy Robinson looked at them for a long time. Then he looked down at his own light brown fur which wasn't shiny any more. He began to feel rather small, and although he was wearing his best purple dress he suddenly felt old and shabby. He looked at Deborah out of the corner of his eye and saw that she too was staring at the teddy bears. He wondered if she thought they were beautiful, and hoped she didn't.

'I think it's rather soppy to be pale blue, don't you?' he said.

'Yes,' said Deborah. 'I'd rather have your colour to live with. Those teddy bears have to look specially beautiful, poor things.'

'Why are they poor things?' asked Teddy Robinson.

'Because they are prizes waiting to be won,' said Deborah. 'You wouldn't like to be a prize, would you?'

'Oh, no,' said Teddy Robinson, and he began to feel sorry for the big pale blue teddy bears, and hoped they hadn't heard him say it was soppy to be that colour.

He began to feel rather small

After they had looked at quite a few other things they decided to spend their last sixpence on another kind of roundabout. This was one where they sat in a little chair with their feet sticking out in front of them; and as they went round and round they seemed to go higher and higher. They both thought it was rather like being in an aeroplane.

'That was nice, wasn't it?' said Deborah, when they got down again. 'I hope you enjoyed it.'

'Oh, yes, I hope I did,' said Teddy Robinson, 'because it was my last ride. But I think I liked Nellie better.'

'So did I,' said Deborah.

And then, just as they were going on their way out, they saw a roundabout with motor-cars and motor-bikes which they hadn't seen before. They stopped to look at it, and Teddy Robinson felt rather sad.

'I never specially wanted to go in an aeroplane chair,' he said, 'but I did want to ride in a motor-car.'

'I haven't any money left for a ride in one of those,' said Deborah.

'I know,' said Teddy Robinson, 'but let's just look at them. Let's choose which one we would ride in if we did have enough money.'

So they walked all the way round, looking at each of the cars in turn, and they both decided that a bright blue one was the nicest.

'If I sat in the front seat,' said Teddy Robinson, 'do you think my paws would reach the driving wheel?'

'I think they might,' said Deborah.

'Couldn't I just try?' he asked. 'Just for a minute?'

'No, I don't think so,' said Deborah. 'Don't worry me, there's a good boy.'

'Oh, no,' said Teddy Robinson, 'I won't worry you. I'll think about it instead.' And he began thinking to himself in a round-and-round sort of way, like this, 'If I could sit *in* it, for only a minute, sit *in* it, a minute, before they begin it, if I could sit *in* it . . .'

'Oh, all right, then,' said Deborah, 'just for a minute. I don't expect the man will mind'; and she lifted Teddy

The wind ruffled his fur

Robinson up and sat him in the front seat of the little blue car.

'Oh, look!' she said. 'Your paws *do* reach the driving-wheel.'

'So they do!' said Teddy Robinson, and he felt very pleased.

Deborah was so busy admiring him that she never noticed that the roundabout was just going to start. She turned round to show Mummy, and at that minute the cars began to move slowly round. Before she had time to lift him off again Teddy Robinson was out of reach, going round and round in the little blue car all by himself.

He sat up very straight with his paws on the driving wheel and felt bigger and better than he had ever felt before. As he went round and round, faster and faster, the wind ruffled his fur and he felt as if he was going for miles and miles all by himself.

Every now and again he saw Deborah, and each time he passed her she waved her hand at him. He didn't wave back because he didn't want to take his paw off the driving wheel. It was so lovely to be really driving a motor-car at last, and all by himself too. He began to feel a little song going round and round in his head as he went round and round on the roundabout:

> 'Here I are, here I are,
>   driving in a motor-car.
> What a clever bear I be.
> Don't forget to wave to me.
> Lucky, lucky Teddy R.,
>   driving in a motor-car!'

And then at last the cars began to go slower and slower until they stopped. Deborah ran to lift him out.

'Oh, Teddy Robinson,' she said, 'I never meant you to have a ride, but wasn't it fun!'

'It was lovely,' said Teddy Robinson, 'and didn't I drive it well? I never bumped into any of the others.'

After that it was time to go home. Teddy Robinson felt so happy and pleased with himself that he even waved his paw to the pale blue bears as he passed their stall on the way out.

'I'm lucky not to be a prize at a fair,' he said to himself. 'In fact, I'm a jolly lucky chap altogether. I may not have learned to play the piano yet, and I still haven't got a satchel or a pair of Wellington boots, but I did ride on a horse, and I *have* driven a motor-car all by myself.'

And that is the end of the story about how Teddy Robinson went to the fair.

5

Teddy Robinson gets Lost

ONE day Teddy Robinson and Deborah and Mummy all went to the shops together.

First they went to the baker's, where there were buns and cakes and loaves of bread in the window. Then they went to the chemist's, where there were soap and scent and face flannels in the window (and a weighing machine in the doorway). And last of all they went to the draper's, where there were socks and gloves and babies' bonnets in the window, and a little bell on the shop door which rang when they opened it and went inside.

Deborah was going to have a new apron bought for her, so she sat Teddy Robinson up on the counter beside a box of darning wools.

'You sit here, Teddy Robinson,' she said. 'You won't be interested in aprons.'

'No, I aren't,' said Teddy Robinson. 'I'll have a look round while I'm waiting.'

So while Mummy held up first one apron and then another against Deborah to see if they were the right size, Teddy Robinson looked all round the shop.

Up above his head there were some brightly coloured ribbons hanging in a line – red, blue, yellow, and pink.

'You sit here, Teddy Robinson'

Teddy Robinson stretched up his head so that he could
see them better, and then, by mistake, he fell over backward and rolled down behind the counter. Nobody saw
him go, so nobody was surprised except himself.

It was rather dark down there, but from where he lay
he could see all sorts of little odds-and-ends of ribbon
and lace and small pieces of paper lying on the floor,

and a little farther along he could see the feet of the shop lady who was busy wrapping up Deborah's new apron.

A moment later he heard Mummy's voice on the other side of the counter saying, 'Good morning. Thank you very much.' Then the shop doorbell rang, and he heard the door close.

That's funny, thought Teddy Robinson, they must have gone without me; and he waited to see what would happen next.

But nothing much did happen for quite a long while. The feet of the shop lady walked away from him and went into a room at the back of the shop, and then everything was quiet.

Teddy Robinson was just thinking it was about time somebody came and found him when the lady came back again. And this time she did see him.

'Well, I never!' she said as she picked him up. 'Whatever are *you* doing here?'

The lady's name was Mrs Jones, and she had a little girl called Linda, and Linda had a teddy bear of her own. So she dusted him carefully and then began to think who he could possibly belong to. But such a lot of people had been in the shop that morning that she couldn't tell which of them had left him behind.

And then in came the little girl, Linda. She had been at school all the morning, but she always came home at dinner-time.

He was afraid Linda might put how much he cost

'Oh! Isn't he sweet!' she said when she saw Teddy Robinson sitting on the table. 'Who does he belong to?'

'I don't know,' said Mrs Jones. 'I found him lying down behind the counter. Some one must have dropped him when they were shopping.'

'What will you do with him?' asked Linda.

'Well, I expect whoever he belongs to will come back,' said Mrs Jones. 'But I thought I might put him in the window so that they could see him if they happened to pass by.'

Teddy Robinson was very pleased when he heard this. He had always wanted to sit in a shop window!

'And we ought to put a notice on him,' said Linda, 'to say that he's lost.'

'That's a good idea,' said Mrs Jones. 'You can write it out for me because I shall be rather busy.'

So after dinner Mrs Jones sat down with a boxful of babies' bootees and gloves, and Linda sat down with a pen and ink and a piece of card.

Teddy Robinson sat by and watched them both. When he saw Mrs Jones writing on the little labels to say how much each pair of bootees cost he was rather worried. He was afraid Linda might be going to put how much he cost on the notice she was writing for him, and although he very much wanted to sit in the shop window he didn't at all want anyone to buy him.

But it was all right. Linda just wrote 'I AM LOST' on the card, and then she showed it to her mummy.

'That is lovely,' said Mrs Jones.

'But he wants it fixed on,' said Linda, 'and I don't know how to do it. He ought to wear the babies' gloves, then we could pin the notice on one of them.'

'Yes,' said Mrs Jones, 'but we can't let him wear these. They are quite new.'

Then she remembered that there was a little pair of blue gloves in the front of the shop window.

'They are a bit faded,' she said. 'I don't suppose anyone will buy them now. And there's a pair of bootees. Run and fetch them, there's a good girl.'

So Linda ran and fetched the blue gloves and bootees from the window and put them on Teddy Robinson. They fitted him exactly, and Mrs Jones and Linda thought he looked so nice in them that they said he could keep them for always.

*He thought
the flies were very rude*

Then they pinned the card on to his left-hand glove and he was all ready to go in the window.

Linda kissed them both good-bye and ran off to school, and Mrs Jones took Teddy Robinson and sat him on a shelf right in the middle of the shop window. Then she unlocked the door and pulled up the little blind to show that the shop was open again for the afternoon.

It was very warm in the window. The sunshine came pouring in, and Teddy Robinson sat looking out on to the street and thought how jolly it was to have such a fine view of everything.

Their noses went quite flat

I wonder who will be the first person to notice me, he thought.

There weren't many people in the street outside because most of them were still at home finishing their dinner, so at first nobody noticed Teddy Robinson except the flies. They began to buzz all round his ears, and then some sat on his nose and tickled him.

'Go away,' said Teddy Robinson.

But the flies took no notice. They buzzed louder.

> 'Buzz! Buzz! Silly old bear,
> what in the world are you doing up there?'

Teddy Robinson thought the flies were very rude so he pretended not to notice them, and after a while they stopped worrying him.

Then an old lady stopped to look in the window. She smiled when she saw Teddy Robinson, and after a moment she put on her glasses and leaned forward to read what was written on his label. When she had read it she smiled again, and nodded her head at him to show that she was sorry he was lost but was sure he would be found again soon.

'That was kind of her,' he said to himself as she went away.

More and more people stopped to look in the window, and when they saw him they smiled and said things to each other, and pointed him out to their children. The children came up close to the window and pressed their faces against the glass and stared. They looked very funny from the inside because their noses went quite flat.

Teddy Robinson began to feel proud because so many people stopped to look at him, and he wished he could hear what they were saying. But he couldn't because of the glass window in between them, so after a while he began making up a little song to himself about what they *might* be saying. It went like this:

> 'Stop! Stop!
> And look in the shop!
> Stare! Stare!
> At the beautiful bear!
> With gloves on his fingers
> and shoes on his toes,
> who *does* he belong to?
> Why, nobody knows!'

And then all of a sudden who should he see but Deborah and Mummy! They were staring in at the window and looking so pleased and surprised! And a moment later the shop bell rang and in they came.

Then Teddy Robinson was lifted down from the window, and Deborah hugged him and admired his gloves and bootees, and Mrs Jones told them about how she had found him under the counter, and Mummy said thank you very much indeed for looking after him so well, and Deborah said thank you for having him, and they all said good-bye.

'Did I look nice in the shop window?' asked Teddy Robinson when they got outside.

'Yes, you looked lovely,' said Deborah.

'I thought perhaps I did,' said Teddy Robinson. 'It was nice being lost, but it's even nicer being found again. Oh, bother! I forgot to say thank you for having me.'

'That's all right,' said Deborah, 'I said it for you.'

Then they all went home to tea.

And that is the end of the story about how Teddy Robinson got lost.

6

Teddy Robinson meets Father Christmas

ONE day Teddy Robinson looked out of Deborah's window and saw that all the trees were quite bare and there was a little pattern of frost on the window-pane.

'I suppose this is winter-time,' he said. 'Br-r-r-r! I'm glad I've got a fur coat.'

'Yes,' said Deborah, 'it's winter-time, and it's nearly Christmas. Shall I sing you a Christmas carol?'

'Yes, please,' said Teddy Robinson. So Deborah sang him the *Rocking Carol*, which begins like this:

> 'Little Jesus, sweetly sleep, do not stir,
> We will lend a coat of fur.
> We will rock you, rock you, rock you.'

'I like that,' said Teddy Robinson. He thought the words were very pretty and wished he could have been there to lend his own coat of fur.

Then Deborah told him all about Father Christmas, and how he would come and fill their stockings with toys on Christmas night.

'We must hang up a stocking for you, Teddy Robinson,' she said. 'I specially want a paint-box in mine. What do you specially want in yours?'

'I don't specially want anything,' said Teddy Robinson, 'except to see Father Christmas when he comes. We shall see him, shan't we?'

'No, I don't think so,' said Deborah. 'Mummy says he never comes unless every one is asleep.'

'But I did see him once, didn't I!' said Teddy Robinson.

'No, you couldn't have,' said Deborah.

'But I did. I'm sure I did. At least, I think I did. Are you sure I didn't?'

'I don't think you could have,' said Deborah.

'Oh,' said Teddy Robinson, 'then I must have dreamt it.' But he still didn't quite believe it.

For the next few days they were very busy making Christmas cards, and choosing presents for people, and learning Christmas carols, and helping to put up the decorations.

Teddy Robinson wasn't very good at learning the carols. Deborah tried to teach him Good King Wenceslas, but he got it wrong every time.

'Try again,' said Deborah.

Teddy Robinson sat up very straight and sang, 'Goofing Wempers Lass Look-out . . .'

'No!' said Deborah. 'That's *wrong.*'

'Well, I think I'm better at making up my own songs,' said Teddy Robinson. 'I'll sing it my own way.'

'Teddy Robin-son look-out
  On the feast of Stephen,
All the stars were round about,
  Some odd ones and some even.'

'No, that won't do at all,' said Deborah. 'I think
we'd better go and help Daddy and Mummy with the
decorations.'

So they did; and after that Deborah went off to wrap
up her Christmas presents and hide them in a secret
place.

Teddy Robinson hadn't any presents for anyone, but
he was very busy making up a Christmas song which he
was going to sing to Deborah on Christmas morning.
So far he had only made up half of it, and when he
couldn't think of the right words he just sang te-tumty-
tum to fill in the spaces. It went something like this:

'Hooray, hooray,
  it's Christmas Day,
  your stocking's full already.
Te-tumty-tum, te-tumty-tum,
  with lots of love from Teddy.'

It's a good idea for a present, he thought, because I
don't have to buy it, and I don't have to wrap it up
and hide it away; I just make it up in my head and keep
it there until Christmas Day. I hope I get it finished in
time, he said to himself.

At last it was Christmas Eve. When bed-time came
Deborah and Teddy Robinson hung up their stockings

They hung up their stockings side by side

side by side. Deborah's was one of her long winter socks, and Teddy Robinson's was one of his little blue bootees.

'We must go to sleep quickly tonight,' said Deborah, 'because it's a magic night.'

So they snuggled down together and lay and thought about Christmas until Deborah fell asleep, and then Teddy Robinson lay and thought about Christmas all by himself.

Much later on Mummy came in quietly to see if Deborah was asleep. She lifted Teddy Robinson out of the bed, kissed him softly on the nose, and then sat

He wanted to see what a magic night looked like

him on the window-sill while she straightened the blankets and tucked Deborah up tidily.

Teddy Robinson was glad he had been put on the window-sill. Deborah had said it was a magic night, and he very much wanted to see what a magic night looked like.

When Mummy had gone he peeped through the curtains and stared out into the darkness. A few lights were still burning in the upstairs windows of the houses near by, but most of the houses were dark because all the people had gone to bed. He watched until one by one the lights had all gone out, and then he stared up into the sky. The stars were there, twinkling and sparkling and winking, just as they had been on the night when he had slept out in the garden. He wondered if they could see him now, peeping through the curtains.

Then the clock in the church tower struck twelve, slowly and clearly. Teddy Robinson counted one, two, three, four, three times over; and then he held his breath and listened. Very faint and far away he thought he could hear the sound of tiny jingling bells.

At the same moment he noticed that the stars seemed to be twinkling much more brightly, and some of them were spinning round, and shooting across the sky, just as if something very exciting was happening up there. The noise of the jingling bells grew louder, as if it was coming nearer, until soon all the air seemed to be filled with the sound.

And as Teddy Robinson sat there watching the stars spinning and listening to the music of the bells ringing he suddenly remembered that he *had* seen Father Christmas. Long, long ago, when he was a new little teddy bear, it was Father Christmas who had brought him to Deborah's house. They had come swooping through the sky in a sleigh pulled by reindeer, and the stars had all to shoot out of their way because they were travelling so quickly, and the sleigh bells were all ringing just as they were now.

He began to feel excited and happy, and a little song began to make itself up in his head:

> Magic night,
> magic night,
> all the children tucked up tight.
> Father Christmas on his way,
> driving in his magic sleigh.
> Toys he brings,
> and dolls and things,
> and every silver sleigh bell rings,
> While down below a brown bear sings —

Before he could get any further a draught of cold air blew the curtains inward, and Teddy Robinson fell backward off the window-sill and rolled over on to his back on the carpet.

And there in the middle of the room stood Father Christmas!

Teddy Robinson was so surprised that he just lay on his back and stared. Father Christmas smiled, and picked him up, and laughed quietly as he stroked his ears.

'Hallo, Teddy Robinson,' he said. 'Did I give you a surprise? Do you remember me?'

'Yes, I do now,' said Teddy Robinson. 'You're Father Christmas, and you brought me here when I was new. I suddenly remembered when I heard the sleigh bells ringing.'

'That's right,' said Father Christmas. 'You were a

new little bear then; I can see you are older now, but you still look just like Teddy Robinson. Are you happy here with Deborah?'

'Yes, very happy.'

'Good,' said Father Christmas. 'I chose you for her because I knew she would love you. Do you remember the night I brought you here?'

'I only half remember it,' said Teddy Robinson. 'It seems like a dream I once had. Do tell me about it.'

'All right,' said Father Christmas, 'but first I'd better fill Deborah's stocking.'

'Have you brought her a paint-box?' asked Teddy Robinson.

'Yes, and I've brought her a drawing book and some pencils to go with it,' said Father Christmas.

'That's good,' said Teddy Robinson. 'Her old ones are all blunt, and they're too short to draw with. What else have you brought her?'

'Oh, all sorts of little surprises,' said Father Christmas, 'but you'll have to wait till the morning to see them.'

Then he opened his big sack and brought out a lot of little parcels all tied up in different coloured papers with gold and silver string, and he packed them into Deborah's stocking as tightly as they would go. When at last the stocking was full right up to the top he looked at Teddy Robinson's little blue bootee.

'That's mine,' said Teddy Robinson, 'but you don't have to put anything in it.'

'No,' said Father Christmas, 'but I will, all the same. Promise not to look.'

So Teddy Robinson promised and stared hard at the ceiling while Father Christmas filled his blue bootee with a string of beads, a lollipop, two pattypans, and a cracker.

Then he bent over to look at Deborah, kissed her gently on the cheek, and came back to Teddy Robinson.

'Now,' he said. 'I'll tell you about the night I brought you here,' and he sat down on the low chair by the window and took Teddy Robinson on his knee.

'It was Christmas night, of course,' said Father Christmas, 'and we started off with a sleigh full of toys. You were near the top of the sack because you specially wanted to be near a little toy horse called Cloppety –'

'Oh! I know him!' said Teddy Robinson. 'I met him in hospital.'

'Did you, now!' said Father Christmas. 'I remember I was taking him to a little boy called Tommy.'

'Yes, I know him as well,' said Teddy Robinson.

'Fancy that!' said Father Christmas. 'Well, that night we went so fast that the sack came undone and you nearly fell out. So I brought you out and tucked you inside my big red coat, with only your nose and eyes peeping out.

'We went rushing along, and the stars had to keep

shooting out on either side of us to get out of our way, and you kept peeping out over the edge of my coat and saying, "Oh, my! Oh, my! We *are* up high!" Dear me, you *did* enjoy that ride!'

'I bet I did,' said Teddy Robinson, and he felt his fur tingling with excitement. 'Go on telling me.'

'There isn't much more to tell,' said Father Christmas; 'it was a long ride, and as we began to swoop down towards the earth you began to get sleepy. We passed over the tops of some fir-trees, I remember, and woke up some birds who were sleeping on a branch, and then we saw the roofs and chimney pots of the first houses, and then, as you were only a very new little bear, you began to get sleepier and sleepier, and by the time we got here to Deborah's house you were sound asleep.'

'I think I remember now,' said Teddy Robinson. 'I hope I don't forget again before next Christmas.'

'I don't think you will,' said Father Christmas, 'because I have got a present in my pocket that I think will just fit you, and I hope it will make you always remember me. Shall I give it you now, or shall I put it in your stocking?'

'I'd like it now, please,' said Teddy Robinson.

So Father Christmas felt deep down in the big red pocket of his big red coat, and he brought out a beautiful little collar made of red leather with a shiny silver bell fastened on to the front of it.

'I made it myself,' he said. 'I was making some new

'Now hop into bed like a good bear'

reins for the reindeer, and when I had finished there was one little strip of leather left over, and one little silver bell, so I made it into a collar.'

Then he fastened it round Teddy Robinson's neck and Teddy Robinson was so pleased he hardly knew how to say thank you. Every time he shook his head the little bell tinkled.

'And now I must be off,' said Father Christmas. 'Lots

and lots of empty stockings are waiting to be filled, and it's high time all teddy bears were asleep.'

'Couldn't I come with you?' asked Teddy Robinson.

'What! And leave Deborah?' said Father Christmas.

'No, I suppose not,' he said. 'I was only thinking I *would* like another ride with you. Where is your sleigh now?'

'In the garden,' said Father Christmas. 'Now I must fly; so hop into bed like a good bear, and I'll tuck you up before I go.'

'I haven't learned to hop yet,' said Teddy Robinson.

'No, of course not,' said Father Christmas, 'and I haven't learned to fly. I only meant it's time for me to go, and time for you to be in bed.'

Then very gently he tucked him in beside Deborah, whispered 'Happy Christmas,' and a moment later there was a jingling of bells, a soft swishing noise outside the window, and then everything was quiet. Father Christmas had gone.

Teddy Robinson lay in the dark and thought how lovely it would have been to have sent the stars spinning and to go rushing through the sky to the North Pole with the wind whistling through his fur, and the little silver bell on his collar ringing with all the sleigh bells.

But then he saw the knobbly shape of Deborah's stocking hanging by the bed, and the smaller knobbly shape of his own stocking hanging beside it. He felt the ends of Deborah's hair tickling his ears as he cuddled down beside her, and he knew that Father Christmas had been quite right to leave him there. He didn't ever want to live anywhere else in the world except in Deborah's house.

And that is the end of the story about how Teddy Robinson met Father Christmas.

7

Teddy Robinson has a
Birthday Party

ONE day Teddy Robinson said to Deborah, 'You know, I've lived with you for years and years and years, and yet I've never had a birthday. Why haven't I?'

'I suppose it's because you came at Christmas,' said Deborah, 'so we've never thought about it. Would you like to have a birthday?'

'Oh, yes, please,' said Teddy Robinson, 'if you can spare one. And can I have a party?'

'Yes, I think it's a lovely idea,' said Deborah. 'When would you like your birthday to be?'

'Today?' said Teddy Robinson.

'No, not today,' said Deborah. 'There wouldn't be time to get a party ready. I shall have to ask Mummy about it. Besides, I haven't got a present for you.'

'Tomorrow, then,' said Teddy Robinson.

'All right,' said Deborah. 'We'll make it tomorrow. How old would you like to be?'

'A hundred,' said Teddy Robinson.

'Don't be silly,' said Deborah. 'You can't be a hundred.'

She made a paper crown for him to wear.

'Why not? I've been here about a hundred years, haven't I?'

'No, of course you haven't,' said Deborah. 'I know it seems a long while, but it's not as long as all that. I think you're about three or four. I'll ask Mummy.'

Mummy thought it would be a good idea for Teddy Robinson to have a party.

'You can ask Philip and Mary-Anne to tea,' she said, 'and I'll make some things for you to eat. Would Teddy Robinson like a birthday cake?'

'Oh, *yes*,' said Deborah, 'with candles on. But how old is he?'

'I think he's three really,' said Mummy, 'but I'm afraid he'll have to be one tomorrow, because there's only one cake candle left in the box.'

So everybody started getting ready for Teddy Robinson's birthday party.

Deborah bought him a little trumpet for threepence and wrapped it up in pink tissue paper. Then she made a paper crown for him to wear on his head (because he was going to be the birthday king). Mummy made the cake, and iced it, and wrote TEDDY on top with tiny silver balls. Then she made a lot of very small jellies in egg-cups. And Teddy Robinson sat and sang to himself all day long, and felt very proud and important, because he was going to have a birthday all of his own.

It was beautifully sunny the next day, so Deborah and Teddy Robinson decided they would have the party in the garden.

'We will have the little nursery-table under the almond-tree,' said Deborah, 'and you shall sit at the head, Teddy Robinson, and wear your purple dress and the birthday crown.'

'Yes,' he said, 'that will be lovely,'

'Now I must find something for us all to sit on,' said Deborah. 'I think my own little chair and stool will do for Mary-Anne and me, and the dolls will have to sit on the benches. Philip can have the toy-box turned upside down.'

'And will there be three chairs for me?' asked Teddy Robinson.

'No, not *three*,' said Deborah. 'Why ever should you want three?'

'But don't they always have three chairs for some-body special?'

admiring the birthday cake

'Oh, you mean three *cheers*,' said Deborah. 'That means three hoorays.'

'Oh,' said Teddy Robinson; 'then can I have three hoorays if I can't have three chairs?'

'Yes, I expect so,' said Deborah. 'Now, don't interrupt me, because I want to get everything ready.'

So Teddy Robinson sat and watched Deborah putting the chairs and benches out, and began singing his three hoorays, because he was so happy and excited.

> 'Hooray, hooray, hooray,
> my birthday party's today.
> You can come to tea
> at half-past three,
> and stay for ever, hooray.'

'Oh, don't say that,' said Deborah. 'It will all have to be cleared away and washed up afterwards, so we can't have people staying for ever.'

'All right, then,' said Teddy Robinson:

'Hooray, hooray, hooray,
my birthday party's today.
You can come to tea
at half-past three,
and stay until we tell you to go, unless somebody's
    fetching you.'

'Is that better?'

'Yes,' said Deborah, but she wasn't really listening, because she was so busy thinking about where everybody was going to sit, and what she should use for a tablecloth, and whether there would be enough cups and saucers.

At half-past three the visitors arrived. The dolls were already sitting in their places, admiring the birthday cake with its one candle, and the little jellies, and the chocolate biscuits, and the piles of tiny sandwiches that Mummy had made.

And Teddy Robinson, wearing his best purple dress and his crown, was sitting on a high stool at the head of the table, and feeling like the King of all teddy bears.

'You do look grand,' said Philip. 'May I sit beside you?'

'Oh, yes,' said Teddy Robinson, and felt very pleased at being asked. Philip gave him a small tin cow and some dolly mixture in a match-box for his present.

'Oh, thank you,' said Teddy Robinson. 'I love cows, and Deborah loves dolly mixture. That *is* a good present.'

Nobody minded her eyes being shut.

Mary-Anne had brought Jacqueline with her. Jacqueline was her beautiful doll, who wore a pink silk dress and a frilly bonnet to match. Teddy Robinson was suprised to see that Jacqueline's eyes were shut, although she wasn't lying down.

Mary-Anne said, 'Many happy returns of the day, Teddy Robinson. This is Jacqueline. Her eyes are shut, because she's rather tired today.' ('They're stuck, really,' she whispered to Deborah.) 'But she is *so* looking forward to the party.'

Jacqueline had such a beautiful smile that nobody minded her eyes being shut, and Teddy Robinson was very pleased when she was put to sit on his other side at the table.

'And this is Jacqueline's present to you,' said Mary-Anne, and she put a little parcel down on the table in front of him. Inside was a beautiful little paper umbrella.

It was red with a yellow frill all round the outside edge.

Teddy Robinson was very pleased indeed. 'It's just what I was wanting,' he said. 'Can I have it up now?'

'Yes,' said Deborah, 'it can be a sunshade today.' And she opened it up for him. With a sunshade as well as a crown, Teddy Robinson felt grander than ever.

They had a lovely tea. Deborah poured the milk into the dolls' cups and saucers while Mary-Anne handed round the sandwiches, and Philip made everybody laugh by telling them funny stories.

Every time Teddy Robinson laughed he fell sideways against Philip, and his crown went over one eye, and this made every one laugh more than ever.

'Don't make him so excited,' said Deborah. 'You're

every time he laughed he fell sideways

It seemed rather a waste to put all round the table edge.
'Oh dear! It isn't very nice,' she said to herself. She just
then was wondering about it and ...

'I feel just like standing on my head.'

making him behave badly.' But Teddy Robinson just
got jollier and jollier. He was having a wonderful time.
He began singing:

> 'Ding, dong,
>   this is the song
> I'll sing at my birthday tea.
> I'm glad you came,
>   but all the same,
> the party's really for me. . . .'

'Teddy Robinson!' said Deborah. 'What a rude thing
to sing to your visitors!'

'Oh, sorry!' said he. 'I didn't really mean that. All
right, I won't sing. I'll ask you a riddle instead. When
is a bear bare?'

'What does it mean?' asked the dolls. 'It doesn't make
sense.'

'When he's got no fur on!' said Teddy Robinson, and laughed until he fell sideways again. As nobody else understood the riddle they didn't think it was funny, but they laughed like anything when Teddy Robinson fell sideways, because his crown fell over his eyes again, and the umbrella came down on top of his head.

When it was time for the birthday cake everyone sang *Happy Birthday to You*, and just for a minute Teddy Robinson forgot to feel jolly, and felt rather shy instead. But as soon as they had finished he got jollier than ever.

'I feel just like standing on my head,' he said.

'Go on, then,' said Philip. 'I'll help you.'

'No, don't,' said Deborah. But Teddy Robinson was already standing on his head in the middle of the table with Philip holding on to him.

'Well done!' shouted Philip, as Teddy Robinson's fat, furry legs wobbled in the air. All the dolls laughed except Jacqueline, who couldn't see, because her eyes were shut, but she went on smiling all the time.

'Now I'll go head-over-heels!' said Teddy Robinson, and over he went.

'Mind the biscuits!' cried Mary-Anne, and took them away just in time as Teddy Robinson came down with a bump that clattered all the cups and saucers. Everybody laughed and clapped except Deborah, who didn't like to see Teddy Robinson getting so rough.

'Do be careful!' she said. 'Philip, put him back on his stool. Teddy Robinson, you really mustn't behave like that.'

'All right, I won't do it again,' said Teddy Robinson. 'I'll sing about it instead.' And then he began singing in a silly, squeaky little voice:

'The Birthday Bear,
the Birthday Bear
stood on his head
with his legs in the air,
and every one laughed
as the Bear with the crown
went head-over-heels
like a circus clown,
and they laughed and laughed
till he tumbled down.
Hooray for the Birthday Bear!'

He was so pleased with himself when he had sung this little song that he fell over backwards and disappeared out of sight under the table. Deborah pulled him out and brushed the cake-crumbs and dry leaves and little bits of jelly off his fur, then she sat him up at the table again.

'Don't be so silly,' she said. 'What ever will your visitors think?'

'They'll think I'm jolly funny,' said Teddy Robinson, 'though as a matter of fact, I didn't mean to fall over at all that time. I just leaned back, and there was nothing

Ex-and-shoff.

behind me, so I fell through it.' Then he began singing
again in the silly squeaky voice:

'Nothing was there,
so the Birthday Bear
leaned back, and fell right through it.
Down with a smack
he fell on his back!
Wasn't he clever to do it?'

Everybody started laughing again at this, so Teddy
Robinson thought he would be funnier than ever. He
leaned sideways against Jacqueline, so hard that she fell
sideways against the doll next to her; and then they
all went down like a lot of ninepins, and fell squeaking
and giggling under the table.

'I'm so sorry,' said Deborah to Mary-Anne. 'I'm
afraid he's a little ex-and-shoff.'

'What is that?' asked Mary-Anne.

'Excited and showing off,' whispered Deborah, 'but
I don't want him to hear.'

'I *did* hear!' shouted Teddy Robinson from under
the table. 'Ex-and-shoff yourself!'

Mary-Anne and Deborah took no notice of this, but
Philip laughed. Deborah said, 'I think it's your fault,
Philip, that he's behaving so badly. You always laugh
when he says something rude.'

They picked up all the dolls from under the table, and
when at last they were all sitting in their places again
Deborah began handing round the chocolate biscuits.

'How dare you sit with your back to the table!'

She put one on each plate, and each doll said 'Thank you,' but when she came to Teddy Robinson's place and looked up to speak to him she found she was looking at the back of his head.

'Teddy Robinson!' she said. 'How dare you sit with your back to the table!'

'I'm not,' said Teddy Robinson in a funny laughing voice.

'You are. Now, don't be so rude and silly. Turn round the other way, and put your feet under the table.'

'My feet *are* under the table,' said Teddy Robinson, laughing more than ever.

Deborah lifted the cloth, and was very surprised to see that Teddy Robinson was quite right. His feet *were* under the table, but his face was still looking the other way, because his head was twisted right round from back to front.

'You *silly* boy!' she said, as she twisted it round again. 'You deserve to get it stuck that way. Now, do behave yourself. You're not being funny at all.'

'*We* think he is very funny,' said one of the dolls politely.

'Thank you,' said Teddy Robinson, and he bowed so low that this time he fell with his nose in the jam, and his crown fell off into the jellies.

'Now,' said Deborah, when they had all finished laughing, 'I think we'd better eat up the rest of the food before any more of it gets spilt or sat on.'

So they finished up all the chocolate biscuits, and all the little jellies, and went on eating until there was nothing left but one tiny sandwich which nobody had any room for. Then, as it was time for the party to end, Philip said:

'Let's have three cheers for Teddy Robinson!'

Every one shouted 'Hip-Hip-Hooray' three times over; and Teddy Robinson bowed again (but this time he didn't fall over) and said, 'Thank you for having me,' because by now he was getting a bit muddled and had forgotten that it was his own party that he was enjoying so much.

And then everybody said 'Good-bye,' and 'Thank you for having me,' and 'Thank you for coming.' and 'Wasn't it a lovely party,' and Philip and Mary-Anne and Jacqueline went home, and the dolls went back to the toy-cupboard, and the party was really over.

Teddy Robinson, tired and happy, lay on the grass beside his birthday crown and umbrella. Deborah picked him up and carried him into the house.

'Well, Teddy Robinson,' she said, 'I hope you enjoyed your birthday party?'

'Oh, yes! It was the best one I ever had.'

'It's a pity you didn't behave a *little* bit better,' said Deborah. 'You're getting a big boy now.'

'Yes, but, after all, I *was* only one today, wasn't I?'

'Of *course* you were; I quite forgot!' said Deborah, and kissed him on the end of his nose.

And that is the end of the story about Teddy Robinson's birthday party.

8

Teddy Robinson and Toby

ONE day Teddy Robinson and Deborah were just coming home from the shops when a lady called Mrs Peters came out of her house and gave Deborah a parcel.

'This is a present for your favourite doll,' she said. 'Open it when you get home.'

'Oh, thank you,' said Deborah. 'What is it?'

'It's a surprise,' said Mrs Peters. 'I made it myself.'

Deborah and Teddy Robinson ran home with the parcel.

'It's for you, Teddy Robinson,' said Deborah. 'I know you're not a doll, but you are my favourite, so it must be for you.'

'I wonder what it is,' said Teddy Robinson.

As soon as they got home Deborah undid the parcel. Inside the brown paper there was some white tissue paper, and inside the tissue paper lay a beautiful little ballet frock. It was white, with lots and lots of frills, and instead of sleeves it had shoulder straps with tiny pink roses sewn on them.

'Oh!' said Deborah. 'It's just what I've always wanted – a dress with a skirt that really goes out. Oh, you *are* lucky!'

"I'm not at all sure it's what I've always wanted"

'But I'm not at all sure it's what *I've* always wanted,' said Teddy Robinson. 'I was rather hoping it would be a pair of Wellington boots.'

'But you can't go to a party in Wellington boots,' said Deborah.

'But I aren't going to a party,' said Teddy Robinson.

'Yes, you are,' said Deborah. 'At least, I am. I'm going to Caroline's party this afternoon, and now you've got such a lovely dress you must come too.'

'Was I invited?' said Teddy Robinson.

'Not really,' said Deborah, 'but that's the best of being a teddy bear – you can go to parties without being asked.'

They tried on the dress, and it fitted Teddy Robinson perfectly. As soon as he saw the frilly skirt standing out all round him he felt so dainty and fairy-like that he forgot to be sorry any more that his surprise hadn't been a pair of Wellington boots.

'I see what you mean about a skirt that goes out all round,' he said. 'It does make you feel like dancing. Do you think if I practised I could learn to stand on one leg like a real ballet dancer?'

'I think you might,' said Deborah. 'Lean up against the window and see.'

So Teddy Robinson stood on one leg, propped up against the window, and spent the rest of the morning thinking about how nice it was to be a ballet-dancing bear with roses on his braces. He rather hoped that people going by in the road outside might look up and see him.

'Perhaps they will think I am a famous dancing bear already,' he said to himself, and he began making up a little song about it.

> 'Look at that bear
> in the window up there
> with the roses all over his braces!
>
> 'You can see at a glance
> how well he can dance,
> and how charmingly pretty his face is!
>
> 'What a beautiful dress!
> I should say, at a guess,
> he has danced in a number of places.'

'But they're not braces,' said Deborah. 'They're

—a ballet-dancing bear with roses on his braces

shoulder straps, and anyway you can't dance as well as all that, even if you are standing on one leg.'

When it was time to get ready for Caroline's party Teddy Robinson suddenly felt shy.

'Perhaps I won't go after all,' he said.

'Why ever not?' said Deborah.

'Well, I do feel a bit soppy,' said Teddy Robinson. 'And I'm so afraid some one may ask me to dance. I haven't really practised enough yet. I wouldn't mind if I had some Wellington boots to wear as well. Nobody would expect me to dance then.'

'But even if you had,' said Deborah, 'you'd have to

leave them in the bedroom with the hats and coats. Nobody ever wears Wellington boots with a ballet frock.'

'Couldn't I stay in the bedroom with the hats and coats?' said Teddy Robinson.

'All right,' said Deborah, 'you can if you want to.'

So when they got to Caroline's house they went upstairs to take off their things, then Deborah went downstairs to the party, and Teddy Robinson stayed sitting on the bed among all the hats and overcoats and mufflers. He recognized some of them and began to feel rather sorry to be missing the party.

'That's Mary-Anne's blue coat with the velvet on the collar,' he said to himself. 'I wonder if she's brought Jacqueline with her.' (Jacqueline was Mary-Anne's beautiful doll.) 'And that's Philip's duffel coat. I shall be sorry not to see him. And that's Andrew's overcoat and yellow muffler. Oh, dear, I wish I'd come in my trousers and braces, or my purple dress.'

Just then there was a scuffling noise outside the door, and Caroline's little dog, whose name was Toby, came rushing into the room and scrambled under the bed.

Teddy Robinson was very surprised. He didn't like Toby much because he was rough and noisy and thought he was a lot cleverer than anyone else. Teddy Robinson wondered whether some one was chasing Toby and waited to see what would happen. But nothing happened. Nobody else came into the room, and Toby

"Are you allowed up there?"

stayed under the bed without making a sound, so after
a while Teddy Robinson forgot about him and began
singing to himself quietly:

> 'Parties are jolly and noisy
>   for children and musical chairs,
> but bedrooms are quiet and cosy
>   for overcoats, mufflers, and bears.'

'Who's that singing?' barked Toby, coming out from
under the bed. 'Oh, it's you,' he said when he saw
Teddy Robinson looking down at him. 'Are you allowed
up there?'

'Yes, I think so,' said Teddy Robinson.

'I suppose it's because you're a visitor,' said Toby.
'I'm never allowed on the beds. But, then, you're only

a teddy bear. I'm glad I'm not a teddy bear. I don't think much of them myself. Caroline has one, but she likes me much better.'

'Yes, but hers is only knitted,' said Teddy Robinson. 'I'm a real teddy bear.'

'Are you?' said Toby. 'I can't see much difference. Why are you wearing that peculiar dress?'

Teddy Robinson didn't know what 'peculiar' meant, but he guessed it was something rude, so he said, 'It's not. It's a ballet-dancer's dress, and it's very pretty.'

'It's pretty peculiar, you mean,' said Toby. 'And why are you wearing a ballet-dancer's dress if you're not dancing?'

'I'm resting just now,' said Teddy Robinson.

'Yes, I see you are,' said Toby. 'But why aren't you going to the party?'

Teddy Robinson didn't like to say 'Mind your own business' in somebody else's house, so he didn't say anything. He thought Toby was very rude and wished he would go away. But Toby went on talking.

'I think it's silly,' he said, 'to come to a party all dressed up, and then to stay upstairs on the bed.'

'And I think it's silly to leave a party and come upstairs to go *under* the bed,' said Teddy Robinson. 'Why are you hiding?'

'I shan't tell you, unless you'll tell me,' said Toby.

'All right,' said Teddy Robinson. 'You say first.'

'They're going to have crackers,' said Toby, 'and I don't like the noise.'

'Oh, I love things that go off with a bang!' said Teddy Robinson.

'Then why are *you* up here?' said Toby.

'I was afraid they might ask me to dance,' said Teddy Robinson.

Just then Deborah came running in, all excited.

'Teddy Robinson, you must come down!' she said. 'We're having tea, and we're going to have crackers, and I've told everybody about your ballet frock, and they all want to see it.'

'All right,' said Teddy Robinson, 'but they won't ask me to dance, will they?'

'No,' said Deborah. 'You can just sit beside me and watch the fun.'

So Teddy Robinson went down with Deborah, and everybody admired his ballet frock and made a fuss of him, and as nobody asked him to dance he sat beside Deborah at the table and felt very happy and pleased to be there after all.

When they pulled the crackers and they went *bang! bang! bang!* Teddy Robinson thought about Toby the dog hiding under Caroline's bed, and felt rather sorry for him.

But it serves him right, he thought. He was very rude to me, and, after all, I was a visitor, even if I wasn't invited.

One of Deborah's crackers had a tiny little silver shoe inside it. She hung it on a piece of ribbon and tied it round Teddy Robinson's neck. Then she gave him all the cracker papers and the little pictures off the outsides of the crackers, and Teddy Robinson sat on them to keep them safe. He had a lovely time.

After tea, when the children got down to play games, Teddy Robinson was put to sit on top of the piano so that he could watch all the fun.

They played Blind Man's Buff, and Squeak, Piggy, Squeak; and then Caroline's auntie sat down at the piano and said, 'Now we'll have Musical Bumps, and there'll be a prize for the last person in.'

This was very exciting. All the children shouted and laughed and jumped while Caroline's auntie played the piano very loudly. Then she stopped suddenly, and all the children had to sit down very quickly on the floor. Whoever was the last to sit down was out of the game.

The louder Caroline's auntie played the more the piano shook, until Teddy Robinson, sitting on top of it, felt he was simply trembling with excitement. The children went *jumpety-jump*, and Auntie went *thumpety-thump*, and Teddy Robinson went *bumpety-bump*, until at last only Philip and Caroline were left in the game. All the other children were sitting on the floor watching.

'This is the last go!' said Auntie, and she began playing *Pop goes the Weasel*. When she got to the 'Pop!' she went *crash* on the piano with both hands and stopped

the wonderful jump

playing. At the same minute Teddy Robinson bumped so high off the piano that he fell right in the middle of the carpet.

Philip was so surprised that he forgot to sit down at all. Every one clapped their hands, and Auntie said, 'Well, done Teddy Robinson! I really think you ought to have the prize. That was a wonderful jump, and you certainly sat down before Caroline did.'

Caroline said, 'Yes, Teddy Robinson ought to have the prize.' And every one else said, 'Yes! Yes! Teddy Robinson is the winner!'

So Caroline's auntie gave him the prize, which was a giant pencil, almost as tall as himself. Teddy Robinson was very pleased.

After that the children all went off to a treasure hunt in the dining-room. Teddy Robinson sat in the big arm-chair and waited for them. He had a paper hat on his head, the silver-shoe necklace round his neck, his giant pencil on his lap, and the pile of cracker papers all round him. He was feeling very happy.

In a minute the door opened a little way and Toby's nose came round the corner, very close to the floor.

'Have they finished the crackers yet?' he asked.

'Yes,' said Teddy Robinson. 'You can come in now. They're having a treasure hunt in the dining-room.'

'Oh, *are* they?' said Toby, and his nose disappeared again very quickly.

'Well, now,' said Teddy Robinson, 'I wonder why he rushed away like that. I told him it was quite safe to come in.'

In less than two minutes Toby was back, but this time he didn't just poke his nose round the door. He came trotting into the room, wagging his tail and holding a little flat parcel in his mouth.

'What have you got there?' said Teddy Robinson.

Toby dropped his parcel carefully on the floor.

'I won it in the treasure hunt,' he said. 'It's chocolate. I'm a jolly clever chap. Those silly children were all looking and looking, but I didn't even bother to look.

"Wherever did you get all those things?"

I just walked in and sniffed my way up to it in a minute. Fancy not being able to smell a bar of chocolate! Don't you wish you were as clever as me?'

'I don't think you've noticed what I've got up here in the chair,' said Teddy Robinson.

Toby stood on his hind legs and looked into the chair.

'My word!' he said. 'Wherever did you get all those things?'

'From the party, before you came down,' said Teddy Robinson. 'These are from the crackers, and this is a little silver shoe, and this is the prize I won for Musical Bumps.'

'Well, I never!' said Toby, looking at him with round eyes. 'You seem to be a jolly clever chap too. I'm sorry I said what I did about teddy bears, and I'm sorry I was so rude about your dress.'

'That's all right,' said Teddy Robinson. 'You were wrong about teddy bears, but, you know, I rather agree with you about the dress. It is a bit soppy. I didn't want to hurt Deborah's feelings by not wearing it, but I'm glad I did now or I shouldn't have come to this lovely party. And now that I've won this very fine pencil I'm not going to bother to be a ballet dancer after all. I shall write a book instead.'

And that is the end of the story about Teddy Robinson and Toby.

9

Teddy Robinson is put in a Book

ONE day Teddy Robinson sat in the bookshelf in Deborah's room. He had his thinking face on and his head on one side, because he was thinking very hard.

Deborah came running in to look for him.

'Where are you, Teddy Robinson?' she said, looking under the bed.

'I'm up here,' he said. 'You can't see me because I'm in the bookshelf, so I probably look like a book.'

Deborah looked up and saw him. 'You don't look like anything but my dear, fat, funny old bear,' she said. 'What are you doing up there?'

'Writing a book,' said Teddy Robinson.

'I don't see you writing,' said Deborah.

'No,' said Teddy Robinson. 'You know I can't write really. But I'm thinking, and it's the thinking that counts.'

'And what are you thinking?'

'Well, I'm thinking that when I've finished thinking it would be nice if you would do the writing for me. You can use the giant pencil that I won at the party.'

'Yes, I will,' said Deborah. 'That's a good idea. Tell me what the book is to be about.'

he just couldn't think what to put in his book

'I don't know yet,' said Teddy Robinson. 'Come
back later, when I've had time to think, and I'll tell
you.'

So Deborah went away, and Teddy Robinson started
thinking again. But he just couldn't think *what* to put in
his book. He thought of all the other people he had seen
writing in books, and he began remembering the sort of
things they mumbled to themselves while they were
writing.

Mummy had a little book that she always wrote in
before she went shopping, and her mumbling went
something like this:

> 'A joint of bread,
> a loaf of lamb,
> a pound of eggs
> and some new-laid jam . . .'

'Well, *that* doesn't make much sense,' said Teddy Robinson to himself. Then he thought about the little book that Daddy sometimes wrote in when he came home at night. His mumbling went something like this:

> 'One-and-six,
> and two to pay,
> add them up
> and take them away ...'

'And that doesn't make sense either,' said Teddy Robinson.

Then he remembered the little book that Auntie Sue used to write in when she was knitting. Her mumbling went like this:

> 'Two for purl
> and two for plain,
> turn them round
> and start again.
> Slip the stitch
> and let it go,
> drop the lot
> and end the row ...'

'That's no good either,' thought Teddy Robinson. 'It must be because they're grown-ups that they write such very dull books.'

So then he thought about the books that Deborah liked to read to him. Their favourite was a book of nursery rhymes.

'All right,' said Teddy Robinson to himself, 'I'll write a book of nursery rhymes. Now, shall I start with

'Baa, baa, brown bear,
    Have you any wool?'

'Twinkle, twinkle, Teddy R.
    How I wonder what you are?'

Just then Deborah came back and said, 'Are you ready yet?'

'Listen,' said Teddy Robinson. 'How do you like this?

'*My* fur is brown, silly-silly.
    Your hair is green.
    When I am king, silly-silly,
    you shall be queen.'

'Who are you calling silly?' said Deborah. 'And my hair isn't green.'

'What a pity,' said Teddy Robinson, 'because I could go on like that for ever.'

'What do you really want to write about?' said Deborah. 'What are you most interested in?'

'Me,' said Teddy Robinson.

'Why, of course,' said Deborah. 'What a good idea! I know what we'll do. I'll put *you* in a book!'

'But would there be room for me between the pages? Shouldn't I get rather squashed?'

'No, I mean I'll make pictures and stories about you and put them in a book: then every one will know about you and think how lucky I am to have such a beautiful bear.'

'Oh, *yes*,' said Teddy Robinson. 'Will you have a picture of me being a pirate?'

'Yes, and I'll tell about how you wanted to go to a party in a ballet frock and Wellington boots.'

Deborah found the giant pencil in the toy cupboard; then she went off to ask Mummy for enough paper to make a whole book. Mummy gave her a roll of drawer-paper.

While Deborah was away Teddy Robinson sat and thought about how jolly it was to be put in a book without having to bother to write it. He began to feel rather important and started talking loudly to the dolls inside the toy cupboard.

'Wait till you see me in a book,' he said. 'Do you wish *you* were going in a book? *My* book is going to be the most beautiful and enormous book you ever saw. It will be made of red leather, with gold edges to the pages, and it will be as big as the garden gate.'

'Don't be so silly,' said Deborah, coming back with the paper. 'It won't be anything of the sort, and you really mustn't talk like that or I shall wish I'd never thought of it. After all, lots of other bears have been in books before. What about Goldilocks? She had three of them.'

'Yes,' said Teddy Robinson, 'but they were only

pretend bears. It's different when you're a real bear. You can't help feeling proud.'

Deborah began to unroll some of the paper and cut it up into pages for the book. But because the paper had been rolled up the pages were all curly and wouldn't lie flat. So Teddy Robinson sat on them to help flatten them out, and while he was waiting he sang a little song to himself, very quietly in case anyone should think he was showing off.

> 'There are books about horses,
> and books about dogs,
> and books about tadpoles,
> and books about frogs,
> and books about children;
> but wait till you see
> the wonderful, beautiful
> Book about Me.'

When the pages were flat enough Deborah folded them together like a real book. But some of them went crooked, so she had to cut the edges. Then the pages seemed too tall, so she cut the tops off them. Then they seemed too wide, so she cut the sides off them. But whichever way she cut them they kept on coming crooked, so in the end the book got smaller and smaller, and still it didn't look like a proper book at all.

'There's just one sheet left,' said Teddy Robinson. 'I'm sitting on it. Couldn't you put me in a newspaper instead?'

...and still it didn't look like a proper book at all.

'No,' said Deborah. 'I want you in a book. I think we'd better go and ask Mummy about it.'

But Mummy was busy hanging up curtains.

'I'm sorry I can't help you just now,' she said, 'but I don't think I should be much good at making a book anyway. Mr Vandyke Brown is the man you ought to ask. He's made lots and lots of books.'

Teddy Robinson and Deborah both knew Mr Vandyke Brown because he lived in their road. He had white hair, and a very large black hat which he always took off whenever he met them out of doors. Teddy Robinson specially liked him because he always said, 'And how are you, sir?' and shook his paw very politely after he'd finished saying 'Good Morning' to Deborah.

'Let's go and see him now,' whispered Teddy Robinson.

'Yes, I think we will,' said Deborah.

So she brushed Teddy Robinson's fur, and off they went.

Mr Vandyke Brown opened the door himself when that rang the bell.

'Good morning,' he said to Deborah. 'What can I do for you? And how are you, sir?' he said to Teddy Robinson, shaking him by the paw.

Deborah told him why they had come, and Mr Vandyke Brown looked hard at Teddy Robinson, with his head first on one side and then on the other. Then he said, 'Yes, I see what you mean. He *would* look nice in a book. Come inside and let's talk about it.'

So they all went indoors into Mr Vandyke Brown's sitting-room, which was very untidy and comfortable. Teddy Robinson sat on a little stool, Deborah sat in a large arm-chair, and Mr Vandyke Brown sat on a table and smiled at them both.

'Am I to do the pictures or the stories?' he asked.

'Well, it would be very nice if you'd do them both.' said Deborah. 'I could tell you the stories if you like.'

'Yes,' said Mr Vandyke Brown, thinking hard. 'Now, what sort of pictures would you like?'

'What sort can we have?' asked Deborah.

'There are all sorts of different ways of making pictures,' said Mr Vandyke Brown. 'I wonder which would be best . . .'

'Ask him what sort of ways,' whispered Teddy Robinson, leaning towards Deborah.

'Teddy Robinson wants to know what sort of ways,' said Deborah.

'Well,' said Mr Vandyke Brown, 'drawing them, or painting them, or embroidering them with wool on cards, or chalking them on pavements, or sticking little coloured pieces of paper on to a bigger piece of paper –'

'I don't think chalking them on pavements would do,' said Deborah, 'because we'd never be able to lift them off. But I think any of the others might be nice.'

—five little pictures of Teddy Robinson—

—one in wool,   *one in chalk,*

V. Brown

'I'll tell you what,' said Mr Vandyke Brown. 'I'll do one of each kind; then you can choose which you like best.'

So Mr Vandyke Brown made five little pictures of Teddy Robinson; one in wool, one in chalk, one with pen and ink, one with paint, and one with little bits of sticky paper.

Teddy Robinson didn't like the sticky-paper one or the wool one because it made him look rather babyish, and Deborah didn't like the chalky one because it made him look smudgy and unbrushed, and neither of them liked the painted one because the colours were so queer. But they both loved the pen-and-ink one because it looked so like him.

'I'm glad you chose that one,' said Mr Vandyke

one with pen and ink,
one with paint,
and one with bits of sticky paper

Brown. 'I hoped you wouldn't choose the painted one, because those are the only colours left in my paint box. All the others seem to have dried up. And I hoped you wouldn't choose the chalky one, because I always get the chalk all over my clothes. And I hoped you wouldn't choose the sticky-paper one, because when I sneeze all the little bits of paper get blown away. And I *am* glad you didn't choose the wool one, because I'm very bad at threading needles.'

Teddy Robinson didn't understand a word of all this but he knew it was his very own book that was being talked about, so he sat quite still and tried to look ordinary. Really he was feeling rather shy. He kept wondering how he ought to look when Mr Vandyke Brown started drawing him.

'Shall I look fierce?'

'Or shall I stand on my head?'

He kept wondering how he ought to look

'Shall I look fierce?' he said to himself. 'Or shall I do something clever, like standing on my head? Or shall I just pretend I don't know he's drawing me?'

'I do want a picture of him with his party face on,' said Deborah.

'Very well,' said Mr Vandyke Brown. 'And while I'm drawing him, suppose you do some drawing too.'

So he gave Deborah a piece of paper and a pencil, and Deborah drew a picture of Mr Vandyke Brown while Mr Vandyke Brown drew a picture of Teddy Robinson. And Teddy Robinson did nothing at all. He decided it would be better if he just went on looking ordinary.

For a whole week after that Teddy Robinson and Deborah went every day to Mr Vandyke Brown's house, and by the end of the week there were pictures of Teddy Robinson lying all over the room, and pages and pages of stories.

'I think we've got enough now to fill a book,' said Mr Vandyke Brown, picking up the pages off the chairs and tables.

'But they're all on different-sized pieces of paper,' said Deborah. 'How shall we sew them together to make a book?'

The picture that Deborah drew

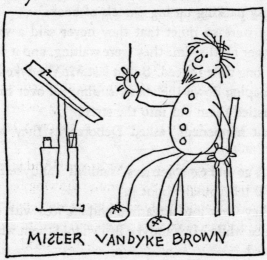

MISTER VANDYKE BROWN

'I don't think we'll bother,' said Mr Vandyke Brown. 'I hate sewing. And, anyway, I've got a better idea. Tomorrow I'll take them all to my friend, the Publisher. He is a very clever man who knows all about how to make proper books. If he likes these he will make them into a real book, so that anyone who wants it can buy it.'

'Can we come too?' asked Deborah.

'I don't see why not,' said Mr Vandyke Brown, 'if Mummy says so. But you'll have to be very quiet and wait downstairs.'

So the very next day Teddy Robinson and Deborah went on a bus with Mr Vandyke Brown all the way to town to see the Publisher. At least Mr Vandyke Brown went to see the Publisher, and Teddy Robinson and Deborah sat downstairs in a large room where a lady was busy packing up big parcels of books.

They were so quiet that they never said a word to each other all the time they were waiting, and it seemed a very long time indeed. But at last Mr Vandyke Brown came leaping down the stairs, smiling all over his face, and hustled them out into the street.

'What happened?' asked Deborah as they hurried along.

'Let's go and eat some ices,' said Mr Vandyke Brown, 'and I'll tell you all about it.'

So they went into a teashop and ate ices with chocolate sauce while Mr Vandyke Brown told them what had happened.

'The Publisher was very kind,' he said. 'He likes the book very much. He laughed in all the right places, and he hopes you didn't hurt yourself, Teddy Robinson, when you fell off the piano.'

'But where is the book?' asked Deborah.

'Oh, it won't be ready for a long while yet,' said Mr Vandyke Brown. 'I'm afraid we shall have to wait weeks and weeks before it is ready. It always takes a long time to make a real book. Is Teddy Robinson disappointed?'

I think he is rather,' said Deborah. 'But never mind.'

'Dear me,' said Mr Vandyke Brown, 'how silly of me not to have thought of it before! Did he think I should come down with the finished book in my hand?'

'He did really,' said Deborah. 'But never mind.'

'Excuse me just a minute,' said Mr Vandyke Brown, and he jumped up and ran to the door. Just outside a lady was selling bunches of violets. Mr Vandyke Brown bought one and came hurrying back. Then he took off his large black hat, bowed low to Teddy Robinson, and gave him the bunch of violets.

'Please accept these with my most grateful thanks,' he said.

Teddy Robinson didn't know what he was talking about, but he was very pleased indeed, because he had never been given a bunch of flowers all of his own, and nobody had ever bowed to him before in quite such an important way.

~pictures of Teddy Robinson lying all over the room.

Weeks and weeks later, when they had nearly forgotten all about it, a parcel came addressed to Master Teddy Robinson, and there inside was *his* book. It wasn't made of red leather, and it wasn't nearly as big as the garden gate, but Teddy Robinson thought it was the nicest book he had ever seen, because it had his very own name on the cover.

And that is the end of the story about how Teddy Robinson was put in a book.

Also in Young Puffin

Joan G. Robinson

TEDDY
ROBINSON
HIMSELF

**Classic stories about a charming teddy bear,
loved for many years by generations
of readers.**

In this book, perfect for reading aloud to young
children, Teddy Robinson meets a mermaid,
comes face to face with a fierce cow and even
tries out a little magic as well as getting involved
in many other adventures.

Joan G. Robinson

KEEPING UP
WITH TEDDY
ROBINSON

**Classic stories about a charming teddy bear,
loved for many years by generations
of readers.**

In this book, perfect for reading aloud to young
children, Teddy Robinson helps some fieldmice
move house, finds himself in the park litter bin
and is sold by mistake in a jumble sale!

The
SNOW KITTEN

This touching story of a little kitten nobody wants is perfect for reading aloud to young children.

Bewildered and hungry, the kitten wandered round the village hopelessly seeking food and shelter until it seemed as if his sad little life would end without ever having properly begun. But the children cared, and tried to work a miracle in time for Christmas.

Also in Young Puffin

LAVINIA DERWENT

The Tale
of
Greyfriars Bobby

Bobby leapt up and licked his hand. He had found his master, that was all that mattered.

The remarkable true story of Bobby, an energetic little Skye terrier, who is devoted to his master Auld Jock. Even when the old man dies Bobby refuses to leave him. Not even the fierce caretaker of the kirkyard can stop him watching over Auld Jock's grave and every night for fourteen years Bobby returns faithfully to sleep by his master.

READ MORE IN PUFFIN

For children of all ages, Puffin represents quality and variety – the very best in publishing today around the world.

For complete information about books available from Puffin – and Penguin – and how to order them, contact us at the appropriate address below. Please note that for copyright reasons the selection of books varies from country to country.

On the worldwide web: www.puffin.co.uk

In the United Kingdom: Please write to *Dept. EP, Penguin Books Ltd, Bath Road, Harmondsworth, West Drayton, Middlesex UB7 0DA*

In the United States: Please write to *Consumer Sales, Penguin USA, P.O. Box 999, Dept. 17109, Bergenfield, New Jersey 07621-0120*. VISA and MasterCard holders call 1-800-253-6476 to order Penguin titles

In Canada: Please write to *Penguin Books Canada Ltd, 10 Alcorn Avenue, Suite 300, Toronto, Ontario M4V 3B2*

In Australia: Please write to *Penguin Books Australia Ltd, P.O. Box 257, Ringwood, Victoria 3134*

In New Zealand: Please write to *Penguin Books (NZ) Ltd, Private Bag 102902, North Shore Mail Centre, Auckland 10*

In India: Please write to *Penguin Books India Pvt Ltd, 706 Eros Apartments, 56 Nehru Place, New Delhi 110 019*

In the Netherlands: Please write to *Penguin Books Netherlands bv, Postbus 3507, NL-1001 AH Amsterdam*

In Germany: Please write to *Penguin Books Deutschland GmbH, Metzlerstrasse 26, 60594 Frankfurt am Main*

In Spain: Please write to *Penguin Books S. A., Bravo Murillo 19, 1° B, 28015 Madrid*

In Italy: Please write to *Penguin Italia s.r.l., Via Felice Casati 20, I-20124 Milano.*

In France: Please write to *Penguin France S. A., 17 rue Lejeune, F-31000 Toulouse*

In Japan: Please write to *Penguin Books Japan, Ishikiribashi Building, 2-5-4, Suido, Bunkyo-ku, Tokyo 112*

In South Africa: Please write to *Longman Penguin Southern Africa (Pty) Ltd, Private Bag X08, Bertsham 2013*